For Ivan and Frances — S. M.

Brimming with creative inspiration, how-to projects, and useful information to enrich your everyday life, Quarto Knows is a favourite destination for those pursuing their interests and passions. Visit our site and dig deeper with our books into your area of interest: Quarto Creates, Quarto Cooks, Quarto Homes, Quarto Lives, Quarto Drives, Quarto Explores, Quarto Gifts, or Quarto Kids.

A catalogue record for this book is available from the British Library.
ISBN 978-1-78603-557-8
The illustrations were created digitally
Set in Archer Pro
Published by Katie Cotton
Designed by Karissa Santos
Edited by Katie Cotton
Production by Jenny Cundill

Manufactured in Guangdong, China EB032020
1 3 5 7 9 8 6 4 2

Kites

Frances Lincoln
First Editions

Simon Mole

Oamul Lu

The day that David moved to Fivehills,
the first thing he noticed was the kites.
Little kites, big kites,
eagle kites, pig kites,
golden frog kites with car headlights for eyes,
mirror kites singing the sky back at itself.

Everybody here had a kite.
Except David.

None of David's things looked quite right in the new house.
His favourite books were lonely on the big bookcase;
his best cars had forgotten how to drive.

But at the bottom of his suitcase,
David found his Grandpa's lucky feather.

Grandpa was a mechanic.

When something broke he always said the same thing:

"Let's see what we've already got.

More often than not, we'll find the answer inside."

David had helped him take apart toasters,
televisions, even a motorbike engine,
using cast-off parts to build
all sorts of awesome adventures.

Grandpa was far away now though,
and what David needed most was a kite.
"Let's see what we've already got..."

"Right!"

Cut, cut, stick.
Cut, cut, tuck, stitch.

Does every pillow
need a case?

Will these old trainers
miss their laces?

Surely every dinosaur would
love to see its tail fly?

Fold, fold, flip.
Fold, fold, hold, lift.

"Yes! Finished! That's it!
I think."

Even from the bottom of the hill,
town was tiny,
and in the sky above it,
like a dream that it was having,
kites of all shapes and sizes,
chasing, diving,
playful in the fierceness of the wind.
David couldn't wait to join in!
He lifted his kite to launch it and...

"Are you new here?"
The girl's voice was light, and fizzy.
"Nice tail," she said. "It looks all... cuddly!"

"But if you want a
breeze-busting, gale-sailing
Wind Wizard of a kite, then you'll
probably need a longer string."

The little girl helped David fix the
new string on as best he could.

"Looking good!"

But before they were even halfway up the hill...

"Is he new here?" The boy's voice was loud and lively.
"Yes!" said the little girl. "He is!
We're going to fly his kite for the first time!"

"Nice string!" said the boy. "Sparkly!
But if you want a cloud-catching, tree-leaping,
whooshing Wind Wizard of a kite, then you
should definitely think about a new frame."

David liked his stripy straws,
Grandpa would have said they did the job just fine. But...

"Yes!" whooped the little girl. "High five!"
That tingle, that zip.
It was time to do the first flight together!
David lifted his kite to launch it and...

"Is he new here?"
The big girl's voice made David jump.
"Err... yeah," said David. "I am. We're just about to
fly my kite, for the first time!"
"What a frame!" said the big girl,
"and that sparkly string!"

"But, you know, if you want a rainbow-racing, sky-striping, whizzing, whooshing Wind Wizard of a kite, then you need to do some work on the colours. I can do a re-spray if you like?"
So David watched open-mouthed
as his kite became...

"Awesome!" said the little girl.
"Awesome!" said the boy.
"Yes!" said the big girl. "A kite has to feel right
for it to fly and now your kite feels right. Right?"

"We can all do the first flight together!"
So David held the kite high
and waited for lift off...

But his kite didn't breeze-bust or gale-sail.
It didn't sky stripe or cloud catch.
It stuttered...

it hiccupped...

it squirmed...

then flopped to the ground,
where it skidded a bit and stopped.
"Maybe kites aren't for me," said David.
He scooped up his sadness and
carried it off to his new house.

His best cars had been parked in a box, and pushed far under the bed.
His favourite books had huddled up together at the end of one shelf.
David knew just how they felt. He buried his head in his pillow
and tried to think about anything but kites.

Then he felt something scratchy, pricking his cheek.
"Let's see what we've already got.

More often than not, we'll find the answer inside."
The feather!

David rushed back over to his kite.

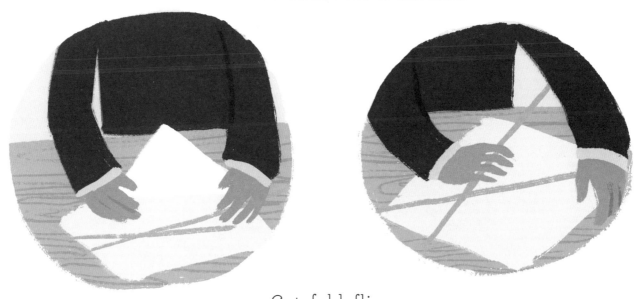

Cut, fold, flip.

Hold, stitch, tuck, lift.

"Yes! Finished! That's it!
That's definitely it!"

David knew the way back to the hill himself.
Soon he found that he was running.
But when he reached the top,
legs tired, chest hammering,
the hill was empty
and the sky was getting darker.
It had to be now.

David blew on the feather once,
a gentle breath of good-flight courage,

then held his kite high and...

Legs light, belly fireworks,
he felt it begin to be tugged up away,
the wind calling it,
quick lift, soar & dip,
his own kite glowing as it rose.
His kite was dancing...

But on its own.

Then another kite blinked on
next to his,
sparkling,

and then two more as if to answer it.

The sky still a vast abyss,
dark and big,
but starred by four kites now.

Each dancing in its own way and together.

David heard his friends' voices as they rushed across the hilltop towards him.

"Now that's a whizzing, whooshing Wind Wizard of a kite!"

David grinned. "It's like you said. A kite has to feel *right* for it to fly."

Simon Mole is the poet from the pub, that rapper from the beach, the friendly guy with the big eyes who told that story. His infectious enthusiasm for seeing and re-seeing the world around him is an open invitation for you to do the same. Simon's groundbreaking one-man show *Indiana Jones & the extra chair* sold out two London runs and toured nationally, while his second, *No More Worries*, toured nationally in 2015 – reaching over 1200 people at 9 venues, including Latitude and Wilderness festivals. His first theatre piece for children, *Friends For All*, was commissioned by the V&A in 2016 and has since toured around England. He has a vast amount of experience across the UK, creating workshops for schools, Pupil Referral Units, museums, prisons, and hospitals. *Kites* is his first picture book. Simon lives in Maidenhead, Berkshire.

Oamul Lu is an illustrator and animator who was born – and still lives today – in China. His art depicts the world he sees, hears, and experiences in daily life, and he hopes that people will be inspired to live their own wonderful life by his artwork. His other picture books include *Held in Love* and *Snowy Farm*.